For Sheila

First published in 1989 by Aurum Books for Children, London
Library of Congress catalog card number: 89-85800
Published simultaneously in Canada by Harper & Collins, Toronto
Printed in Hong Kong
First American edition, 1990

A Piece of Luck

Simon Henwood

Farrar, Straus and Giroux

New York

Once upon a time a man found a piece of luck.

His luck was very rare and special.
It glowed like gold.

At first he kept his luck carefully…

…and when people saw what he had found they were happy for him (even though some of them needed a little luck themselves).

The man's luck grew. Soon he had too much
to handle, so he built a little cart to carry it
all around.

He trundled his good fortune everywhere he went,
but now people became sick of the sight of him.

"Why should one have so much good fortune, while others have none," they complained.

It seemed that the man had all the luck in the world, for there was not one other piece in the whole village.

Now the man was becoming
greedy, and did not wish to
share his fortune with anyone
else. So one night he decided
to take his luck to the top of
the highest hill, where nobody
would be able to steal it.

As the man pushed his cart up the hill, the wheels began to buckle under the weight of all his good fortune, but he carried on anyway.

The greedy man pushed his luck too far. He lost control of the little cart and could not stop it tumbling off the side of the hill with all his good fortune inside.

When the cart hit the ground it broke into a million pieces, scattering good luck throughout the village.

That night many people were fortunate
to find a piece.

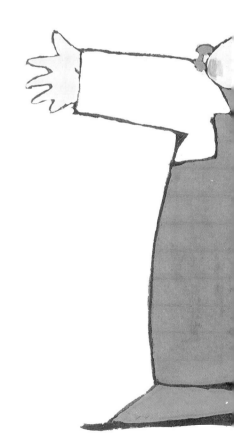

The greedy man, however, searched for days after but, sadly, the only piece of luck he found was quite rotten.